T0005797

With or Without Angels

DOUGLAS BRUTON

Fairlight Books

First published by Fairlight Books 2023

Fairlight Books
Summertown Pavilion, 18–24 Middle Way, Oxford, OX2 7LG

A CIP catalogue record for this book is available from the British Library.

1 2 3 4 5 6 7 8 9 10

ISBN 978-1-914148-36-1

www.fairlightbooks.com

Printed and bound in the Czech Republic by Finidr

Designed by Becca Blackmore-Dawes

Il Mondo Nuovo [*The New World*], Giandomenico Tiepolo, 1791

The Writer's Prologue

(from the Greek 'prologos' meaning 'speaking before')

I am not sure I like crowds. At school once, the playground emptied and I followed all the boys round to the back of the school building. I may have skipped and laughed and thrown my arms above my head. There was some rough exuberance and shouting that sounded like the bellowing of animals – cows in a field once, past milking time, set up such a noise, something pained and plaintive. The very air bristled and thrilled with a boisterous excitement.

Somewhere at the front there was a fight and in a circle about them the press and shove of boys with no pity – so many boys.

At some point I could see blood and I swear I heard the dull thump of a fist against the bleeding boy's cheek, followed by cheering or jeering. It felt like the fight might spill over and all of us be pulled into the punch and kick of it. There was, I think, something animal in that crowd, something sweaty and heaving and feral. I wanted to somehow separate myself from them all and not be any part of it.

It frightened me, stopped my breath or shortened it, and it made my stomach turn.

I remember another time seeing a crowd in the street, all gathered together, their backs turned to me and all their silent focus on something before them that I could not see. Those at the rear and nearest to me stood on tiptoe, craning their necks to better observe what I could not. The people seemed arranged to prevent me seeing, like a wall, and so my curiosity was piqued.

After pushing my way into the crowd, myself on pointe like a dancer and all my body stretched to its fullest reach, I saw that a horse lay dead or dying on the road in front of the people. It was a great sweating lump of toppled flesh, lying on its side with its knobbled legs thrown out straight. Blood leaked from one pink nostril that gaped like an open wound. I held my breath, looking in vain for some sign that the horse still breathed.

A girl at the front retched and threw up beside the dead horse. Someone in the crowd reached forward to pull the girl's hair back from her face, one arm thrown across her hunched shoulder holding her up.

I don't think I had ever been so close to death before. Not such a big death. I remember I was shaking a little and I felt somehow vulnerable, as though Death was part of that crowd, leaning in and silent like the rest of us and somewhere at my shoulder. The sour air smelled of metal and fear and salt. It was the end of something; that much was clear, and as such it was overwhelmingly sad and awful. There were no words and so no one spoke.

Later, I told my mother about the dead horse and the silent crowd. She held one hand over her mouth and her eyes were wide and she pulled me close, held me pressed against her, not letting go.

'I was part of the crowd,' I said to my mother, but I don't think she heard.

*

It is a strange painting. A fresco, really. Cut from the wall of the Tiepolo family villa it had once been in and put in a frame, and now one of the main attractions of the Ca' Rezzonico museum in Venice. It is the work of Giandomenico Tiepolo, son of the greater painter Giambattista Tiepolo. They are both there in the painting, father and son, both dressed in sombre brown frock coats and shown in profile – the son looking over the shoulder of the father, appearing to look through an ocular device like a monocle or a quizzing glass.

The fresco shows a crowd scene but, unusually, the crowd is painted from behind so it is the backs of the people we see painted on the wall and not anything of what they are looking at. They are gathered on the sand where the land meets the sea and beyond them we can see the blue water and where it bleeds into the sky.

Flags like brightly coloured ribbons catch the air.

There are people from all levels of society gathered together: well-dressed ladies with baskets and in one basket a white nesting bird, maybe a dove; and women dressed more roughly; and men in military attire or wearing soft cloth fishermen's caps or the floppy wide-brimmed straw hats of the peasantry or periwigs; and children are there too, and a dog, skinny like a whippet or a greyhound, sheltering at the feet of a tall man in a striking full-length cloak. The clothes of the people are painted in carnival colours, oranges and blues and reds, and despite the beetle-backs and slumped shoulders of some of the onlookers, there is a sense of occasion in the picture, almost a celebration and something of the attendant anxiety that goes with such an occasion.

One man on the left of the picture stands on a high wooden stool. We had such stools, solid and steady, in the art room at school. The man is dressed in a brown coat and breeches with cream-coloured stockings and on his head a cocked tricorne hat from beneath which trails his hair in two pigtails; maybe there is a brown ribbon at the end of each tail. His arms are lifted and he holds a long, thin stick or wand. I do not know what he is doing but he catches our attention and the angle of the raised stick serves to focus our view beyond the crowd to something we cannot quite see.

Between the press of the bodies we catch glimpses of people in masks and costume – the character of Punchinello is there with his tall white conical hat, limp ruff and shiny white satin clothes. This may be the Venice Carnival.

The painting carries the title *Il Mondo Nuovo*: 'The New World'. This could have something to do with a popular entertainment of the day, the term 'The New World' referring to the 'magic lantern' which commonly projected painted glass slides of the New World onto a canvas screen. It may also have something to do with the ending of the Venetian Republic, which had lasted more than a thousand years, or the promise of a new social world order following the French Revolution, or a new more democratic movement in art itself. Maybe it means all of these things or none of them, according to how the viewer chooses to see the work.

The frock-coated father and son do not look to the New World but look across the crowd.

Giandomenico painted other versions of this picture. There is one on canvas in the Prado in Madrid. And another painted onto the walls of the Foresteria (guest house) at the Villa Valmarana near Vicenza. In each version, broadly speaking, we see the same composition with the man in brown (hatless in these two other versions) standing on a heavy wooden stool, his arms raised, and holding the wand at the very same angle as he does in the fresco in Venice.

With these earlier versions we can see the artist working out his thoughts, the Venice fresco reflecting a more mature and complete work.

I have seen parts of the Ca' Rezzonico fresco strikingly reproduced on carrier bags and on bookmarks and on the covers of blank-paged notebooks such as artists might carry.

The First Picture
(Or the Artist's Preface)

He was not well. Something he had eaten perhaps, but there was more than that, too. He told his wife he wasn't feeling strong today, a little uncertain on his feet. She looked disappointed. They had an arrangement. She thought he needed to get out of the apartment, that it would do him good, just to be a step closer to normal. It would do her good also.

He dressed quietly and slowly and he did not allow her to help. She watched him, looked for signs of where the pain was, noticed the way he used his body to soften the hidden smart and sting, but the pain was still there in his face.

'We can go another day,' she said.

He took a breath, drew it deep into his lungs, the bad one and the good. He called for his shoes.

'Only, it might do you some good,' she said, sensing a change in him.

She wrapped a scarf about his neck, soft and thick as a caress.

'It's cold out,' she said.

He put on his coat, buttoned chin to knee, and picked up his stick.

'Right,' he said.

What it was to feel old, he thought. To feel the effort in each breath, the pull and swallow of air, the shortness, the stifling of a cough. There was a stiffness in his back and his legs, and a feeling of everything needing oiled. He straightened and stood tall – not as tall as he'd once stood, nor so straight. He leaned a little heavily on the stick and a little on his small wife.

'Camera?' she said.

He patted his coat pocket, reassured that he had not forgotten the camera. Or maybe she had remembered it and had put it in his coat pocket for him. He wasn't sure. Things were cloudy some days, in his head.

Out on the street the air was wet and chill and shifting. It smelled of bus exhausts and damp wool and faintly of cigarettes. And his wife it smelled of, too. Something with flowers in her perfume. Patchouli maybe – a shrub of the mint family – something of wet soil or apples that are past ripe, the smell of a cork pulled from a bottle of strong red wine. It's the last of the senses to go, smell. He had heard that somewhere and was comforted that when all else failed he would know his wife was at his side by her smell.

He cleared his throat, as though he had something to say, but he lost his place – like reading a book, his finger following under each word and then his hand slipping from the page and the book fallen from his grasp so the covers closed and he did not know where he was in the book and so he had no words to share. She would scold him if she could read his thoughts.

'No, no, no. We'll have no talk of failing and the end of things and closed books and being old.'

She had bought him the camera. He could no longer hold a pen or a brush, at least not for any time. He tucked a pencil behind one ear some days, just to remind himself of what he was, what he had always been. He arranged paper on his desk and ran the flat of his palm across the surface, feeling the soft and familiar velvety burr. There's a smell to paper too, and when he was by himself he leaned in close and breathed that smell in, dry and something sweet and old – he was certain 'old' was a smell.

He took pictures all the time now, arranged like a diary in the memory of the camera. That way he need not fuss over what had happened when. Pictures of meals he ate and people who came to call and paintings he saw in books that meant something. When he later leafed through the pictures he'd taken, he sometimes smiled at the memory; sometimes, too, he puzzled over the picture he'd taken, not understanding why.

'We'll walk a little and then catch a cab. The walk will do us some good.'

He looked up at the sky, still and grey and glowering, like a bad mood that would not be shaken.

He nodded to his wife and made some noise in the back of his throat, a noise that might have been in agreement of what his wife had said about the walk doing him some good, but might just as easily have been something else altogether. She was always so cheery and so positive. It was her strength and she showed him the angels in the world, the angels that he might not have noticed without her.

A bird cut suddenly across the grey above his head. A flash of green and a shriek like a banshee. Improbably, there are ring-necked parakeets in London these days.

*

The Turbine Hall of the Tate Modern gallery on London's South Bank is a great cavernous space. Like a cathedral interior, only more brutally industrial, but no less holy. The ramp that takes you down into the building is open and easy. And light falls through glass from above and from tall windows in the walls at either end.

He knows this space. It is his church. He breathes easier once he is inside and his steps are lighter and he does not lean so hard on his stick, nor need the support of his wife's arm locked in his. He takes the camera out from his pocket, points and shoots.

At the bottom of the ramp there is a mirrored wall or partition. He thinks, at first, that it is a crude and clumsy art installation but it is something put in place by a commercial firm. Maybe it has something to do with further construction work on the building. Maybe it will be part of a promotional presentation for an upcoming exhibition.

He catches his reflection in the mirrored wall. He does not recognise himself. He is greyer and smaller and thinner somehow. He sees his wife on his arm and she looks changed too. Still pretty but the yellow gone from her hair and everything silver now and her eyes, are they still blue? The coat she wears looks too big for her. And caught unawares, she looks tired.

He points his camera and takes a picture. But he is in too much of a hurry and there is a little shake in the picture so that all the edges are softened, like seeing himself and his wife through frosted glass. He takes another picture, the same but different, holds the camera against his chest, holds his breath, holds time suspended – just for the moment it takes for the click of the shutter.

'What is it?' she asks.

'Nothing. It's nothing,' he says. But there is a tremor in his voice and his hand shakes as he lifts the camera to look at the screen on the back. There is the picture he has taken, the picture of himself and his wife standing at the bottom of the ramp in the Turbine Hall of Tate Modern and reflected in a mirrored surface.

He has his stick hooked over his forearm and he stands erect, a little back on his heels, almost as though he is looking up. His wife looks across him and away. Behind them the soft blur of three other people moving past the artist and his wife.

He sucks in air, sharp, as though stung.

She thinks it is the pain in his stomach again and asks him if he wants to sit down. There's a café somewhere with views of the sluggish river and there's tea to be had in thick-lipped cups and cake on small plates.

But it is not the pain in his stomach that has occasioned the sharp intake of breath; no, it is something in the picture the old artist has taken. He does not yet know what it is about the picture that has so stung him, but there is something.

*

His wife sits him at a table and goes to the counter to collect a tray and to make their order. He looks again at the picture of himself and his wife. He wonders what it was she was looking at, what it was she had seen just out of the picture. And maybe it is this that makes him think of a fresco he saw some years ago.

The tea, when it arrives, has a red metallic taste and he wonders if he should add sugar to take the bitter edge off. He should not have declined the cake.

His thoughts drift.

*

He had been in Venice and the air was salted and fresh. He was by himself, with time on his hands. He was just walking, not ever getting lost, for he knows Venice and knows how to locate himself there.

He stopped at a shop that sold paper in all weights and sizes and pencils and sketchbooks small enough to fit in his pocket and decorated with marbled covers. Hanging in the window there were some plastic carrier bags. A picture printed on one caught his eye. It was a small section of an old painting, and it showed a man in a brown coat wearing a three-cornered hat and standing balanced on a wooden stool with a long thin stick in his raised hands. He did not know the painting or the artist, but there was something about the image on the bag that held his attention. It was the colours, like carnival flowers, like a line of laundry he had seen reflected in canal water, the colours seeming to ripple and roll.

He entered the shop, dipping his head to avoid the low stone lintel. It took a moment for his eyes to adjust to the lower light within. On all sides there were buckled shelves, reaching floor to ceiling, stacked with paper and inks and boxes of charcoal.

He asked about the carrier bags in the window. He did not speak Italian, not above a few words, so he could not at first make himself understood. He pointed to the picture on the bag and asked, 'Is this in Venice?' There was space between his words and he gave each word its precise shape and elevated his voice as though he was talking to someone hard of hearing.

The shopkeeper nodded, '*Sì*, in Venice. Ca' Rezzonico.'

He took a water bus. It was only two stops.

Standing in front of the fresco, *Il Mondo Nuovo* by Giandomenico Tiepolo, he was quite breathless and soon a little dizzy. He sat down on the floor in front of the fresco and took it all in. He did not understand what it was he was looking at, but as with any crowd pushing forward to see something strange or wonderful or new, he wanted to peer over their shoulders to see what they were looking at.

*

It is that feeling he remembers now, sitting in the café at Tate Modern looking out through spindle birch trees onto the silted waters of the Thames. The feeling of wanting to know what they were looking at is mirrored in the wanting to know what his wife was looking at in the picture he took at the foot of the Turbine Hall ramp.

But it is something else, too. He sees in himself something of the cloaked figure on the right of the Giandomenico Tiepolo fresco, tall and leaning back a little. It is as though he is on the other side of the crowd, looking now not at their backs but at their faces.

'*Il Mondo Nuovo*,' the old artist says. 'The New World.'

'What?' says his wife.

*

The doctor said it was good news. He said the X-ray showed his lung was clear. The cancer had gone. Of course they would still have to do tests from time to time.

'Perfectly procedural. But for now your cancer has gone. No more treatment. You can go forth and live a long and happy life.'

He laughed; they all laughed.

'The New World,' the old artist said, under his breath so that it was as though he had said nothing at all, as though it was just a thought in his head.

He later prints out the picture taken in Tate Modern's Turbine Hall and pins it to the wall of his studio at home and it nags at his attention, saying over and over, 'Look at me, look at me!'

'We should do something to celebrate,' says the old artist's wife.

He has an idea.

The Second Picture

Sometimes a man can have too many thoughts in his head. That's what the old artist tells his wife when she accuses him of having forgotten to water the plants in the kitchen or leave out money for the window cleaner or call their son. He is like this when he has an idea, when an idea is in his head, walking with him from room to room and ever talking. He's always been like this so he knows it is not an age thing.

When he says 'too many', he is not complaining against the thoughts in his head. There is a thrill in him when he has an idea, when the idea has taken him over and won't let him go. Nor is he complaining against the watering of the plants or the leaving of money for the window cleaner or the making of a call to their son. These things are important too. He knows that.

'Too many' is just a statement of fact and explanation for why he has forgotten these other things. He did not mean to forget, did not want to. But he knows she does not really understand, catches her looking at him, looking for the cracks in his thinking, a little concerned.

When he was physically ill – sometimes the cure can be briefly harder than the illness, it seems – he looked at his life and thought about what there would be of him that survived after he was gone.

She tutted at him then. 'It is too soon for such thinking,' she gently scolded.

The plants in the kitchen would still need watering when he was no longer in the world, but he was certain she would keep that up. And the windows would still need cleaning once a month, so clean that the light seems to fill up the apartment some days, so full you can almost touch the light. And his son and his daughter – she would want to call them from time to time and they'd ask her how she was doing and they would not talk of him, not directly, not with his wife, their mother.

And what of the work – his work? Would it outlast him? Would it have significance and have been worth the time he had given to it? He has doubts. He remembers then something he read about the great man, Leonardo – so great he only needs one name. Each time Leonardo took up a new quill and with the careful edge of his knife – so sharp it could cut air – he carved a new point to the quill, he'd afterwards test the pen not with a small drawing or a few cross-hatched lines of differing thicknesses, but with the writing of a short sentence. It is there in his notebooks, written over and over, surfacing almost as a cry of despair from the thought-filled mind of the great man who left so many projects unfinished (did the ideas in his head make him forget to water the plants, pay the window cleaner, speak to people he loved?): *dimmi, dimmi se mai fu fatta cosa alcuna* – 'tell me, tell me if anything was ever done'.

I think it was Philip Larkin who said something somewhere about what will remain of us when we are gone – and that, he said, is love; love will survive. The words are cut into the stone that remembers Larkin in Westminster Abbey's Poets' Corner, but of the sentiment the old artist is not so sure. It is the work that survives – the finished work and the unfinished – and it is the work that will speak for him long after he is gone. That's what he thinks.

*

You have to spend time with a painting to really understand it. That's also what the old artist thinks. People in galleries – watch them flitting from one picture to the next. They confuse looking with seeing, spending so little time on any individual picture that they miss what the artist wanted to show them. Sometimes there are benches arranged in the centre of the gallery floor. Old men sit there waiting patiently for their wives to be done with looking; or women by themselves sit there, clasping their gallery guides in one hand, pens poised over notebooks filled with small spidery writing and their eyes fixed on one work only, and they are at least trying to see.

Once there was a young woman there, sitting on one of the wooden benches, small and pretty and the sun in her hair. He sat down beside her, close enough he could breathe in the scent of her. He looked to where she looked. If he remembers right it was a blue painting by Yves Klein, a piece of something eternal, and she was lost in the looking, as though she was in the blue or the blue was in her. He took her hand in his – or he imagined he did, for these things are never so simple or so easy. And like that they were both adrift. She smelled of patchouli – did I say that already?

*

The first afternoon the old artist spent at the Ca' Rezzonico museum in Venice he saw only one picture – Giandomenico

Tiepolo's fresco of *Il Mondo Nuovo*, 'The New World'. He wanted to climb up into the picture, to be a part of that crowd – and I am sure that ordinarily and for his own reasons he did not like crowds. He wanted to be pigment and paint and laid down for all time on a piece of wall. His eyes moved through the work, taking in each individual gathered together on Tiepolo's fresco. He imagined himself young, a child running excitedly between the legs of the men in breeches and clutching at the long skirts of the women and stopping to stroke the arched neck of the dog – it was a yellow-brown whippet or a greyhound and a little skittish from his petted attentions. A masked clown glared at him, growled, showing his teeth below a papier-mâché hooked nose with wide nostrils and high rouged cheekbones. The old artist stared so hard at the picture that his eyes stung and began to water.

It was quiet in the gallery room – not that he was entirely alone, but there was a church-hush all about him and the people there talked in hot whispers. He lay down on the floor in front of the picture, closed his eyes and slept.

And the light in the gallery shifted, shadows crawling across the floor towards the far wall.

Suddenly there was noise. Music playing somewhere. Maybe the man on the wooden stool with his arms in the air and holding a long wand, maybe he was conducting some street musicians. He would later pass round his three-cornered hat for the crowd to drop pennies into. And cheering there was, and laughter – though the laughter was far off.

He could smell the perfume of the ladies – something with musk in it and flowers, mint perhaps and the sweetened wet earth mint grows in. And the well-dressed men smelled of rosewater, or those wearing the hats of common men smelled of fish and something sour, too, like meat that has hung too long in the sun or like milk when it has turned and the smell of it when the bottle is raised to the nose makes you jerk back as though stung.

And there were dancers somewhere, dressed in carnival masks, or maybe they were juggling coloured wooden balls and the crowd was held, wanting the balls to clumsily drop and at the same time to stay spinning in the air, birling.

The afternoon sun was high in the sky, and the air sweated and itched.

Then he felt something tugging at his pocket – hadn't they told him that he must be careful of pickpockets? 'They are quick as mice and slippery as eels. You must keep your wallet close and your hand always guarding it.'

'*Signore, signore*, it is done.'

He woke then.

The young gallery attendant was leaning over him, shaking him. There was something gentle in his voice, even tender. Speaking like a lover, almost, and not with any note of censure at this man sleeping at the feet of Tiepolo's *Il Mondo Nuovo*.

'It is time for the gallery to close,' the young man said, smiling.

*

He does not know if when he dreams the pictures in his head have colour. It is strange that as an artist so far on in years he still cannot say. And if they are in colour, he does not know if the colours are true. When he wakes he is left with the memory of those dreamed pictures; they have colour, then. But memory can do that, can add as much as subtract.

'Do you know that when we remember something that was yellow – the fields where we walked as children, the sunlight of those days, or the centres of daisies we made into chains for girls to wear as ragged crowns – the yellow is remembered as something brighter than it was?'

The old artist's wife smiles and nods and says yes, she has heard that.

He looks again at the pictures he took at the bottom of the ramp in the Turbine Hall of Tate Modern. In particular the one of his wife leaning towards him and looking away out of the picture; and himself, tall and on his heels, his walking stick hooked into the crook of his arm and his hands holding the camera, conjuring the picture out of nothing.

'I wonder if we can do something with the background? If we can take the people in the picture and put them in another place? On a seafront beach? In a new world.'

It is as though he and his wife are part of the painting by Tiepolo. That's what he thinks – and the crowd now not seen from behind but from in front. And the strange thing is, the question of what exactly they are looking at remains without an answer.

*

Her name is Olive – Livvy to her friends. He notices the slim long fingers of her hands. And the sun in her hair – didn't his wife have hair like that once? – and the blue in her eyes. The eternal is never really eternal. It is a failure of language. See Yves Klein's blue pictures now and over the fifty years since they were painted they have lost something, he thinks. Maybe it is because they have suffered to be touched and the marks of fingers smear the blue, or the pictures are now behind Perspex or glass and so badly lit that it is hard to see beyond one's own reflection into the forever-blue. His wife's eyes were blue once, are blue still but something less than they were. And now Livvy's eyes are blue, too – a forget-me-not blue that he will one day forget.

Maybe it is something in him that has failed. The old no longer see colours as they did when they were young. There is a deterioration specifically in the perception of blue and yellow. He takes his glasses off and with a cloth from his trouser pocket he rubs at the lenses until he thinks they are clean. Then he replaces his glasses, blinks, adjusting to the newness of the world.

Yes, Livvy has blue eyes. He will not say the blue of her eyes is eternal, but only new.

He coughs, clears his throat and begins to speak. 'It is my hands, you see. It is as though they are not my hands. As though they belong to someone else who has not made art his life's work. I don't know if "art" should have a small "a" or a capital "A". But my hands... well, it is a side effect of the treatment, I cannot hold a pen or a brush – not for the time it takes to make art.'

Livvy nods and looks as though she understands and looks sorry for him.

'My wife bought me this little camera and the pictures I take, some of them are more than pictures; some of them are stories, you see. And so I think I might do something with the pictures – with your help.'

'Of course.'

'But right now it is only an idea in my head – and maybe thoughts have colours and dreams do not. And the thought in my head does not yet have shape or form, only direction, one picture leading into another. It is a journey,' he says. 'And as with some journeys, the destination is not known – except perhaps that in the end we all return to where we started.'

Yes, she can do what he asks, she says, even though she is not certain yet what it is he wants of her.

'Do you know I once fell asleep on the gallery floor in front of Tiepolo's painting *Il Mondo Nuovo*? It was in Venice.'

He laughs and she does too, even though she does not know Tiepolo except as a name and does not know what *Il Mondo Nuovo* means. *Nuovo* translated is 'new', she thinks. But she does not know the word *mondo*.

She puts one hand on his – or he imagines she does.

The Third Picture

Maybe he has it all wrong, Giandomenico Tiepolo's picture: 'The New World'. The crowd turns its back to the viewer of the work, and the viewer some days has been the old artist – when he is not sleeping on the floor in front of the picture. He is not of that world, the world of three-cornered hats and men in breeches and stockings and women with hand-held fans and doves in baskets. He is of this world which may be counted as the new world and the people in the picture turn their backs to him and remain in their own world. Maybe that is what the picture is telling him.

But even as he thinks that, he feels lost, like he does not really belong in the world he walks about in. That he belongs in a world that has already disappeared – a world of three-channel TV and Bakelite phones and cheese wrapped in waxed paper and fish and chips wrapped in yesterday's black-bleeding newsprint. A world of OMO washing powder and Sandie Shaw wearing no shoes and films with intermissions and usherettes selling ice cream and cigarettes. The 'new' in 'new world' is only relative.

*

On the old artist's second visit to the Ca' Rezzonico gallery the young attendant recognised him and nodded and got to his feet and shook his hand. Then reaching under his desk he brought forth a cushion and proffered it to the old artist.

'In case you have the feeling to sleep. The floors are a little... how you say, *duro*, hard.' He mimed laying his head on the cushion and falling asleep. Then he laughed and nodded and pushed the old artist to take the cushion.

On this second visit to the Ca' Rezzonico gallery he saw only the one picture again, the same one. He put the cushion on the floor in front of the fresco and sat.

Behind him an American woman said she thought the people in the picture were rude to turn their backs so. She did not see the point. 'It is called *Il Mondo Nuovo*.' The woman she was with explained that it meant 'The New World'. They were both silent a moment. Then the first woman said she did not get it and they moved into another room in the gallery.

The old artist smiled to himself.

*

He asks Livvy if she can maybe mix two different pictures together, the picture of himself and his wife with another picture of the ramp down to the Turbine Hall. And stairs cut into more stairs by the mirrored reflection. 'And can we put more people in the picture so it is a little crowded?' There is one man in particular he would like to include, right at the front of the picture. The man is a little blurred, like he is moving quickly, like he is not all there, a ghost of a man, his face looking up – at heaven maybe.

'And you should be in the picture, too,' he says to Livvy. 'Looking off to the left, yes, in the opposite direction to where my wife looks. I don't know what that means. And something from Tiepolo should be there, too.'

In the Ca' Rezzonico gallery there are other pictures by Giandomenico Tiepolo. One shows Punchinello in love, his hand pressed to the breast of a masked woman in a feathered hat who is dancing with her arm thrown about the neck of Punchinello. Another shows Punchinello on a swing, a rope strung between two trees and he is high in the air and we are below looking up. And a third carries the title *Punchinello and the Acrobats*. In this third picture Punchinello carries a mini-Punchinello in his arms, a child-Punchinello. The old artist thinks there is room in his photograph for these two Punchinello figures, a little hidden so they could be missed.

'So that you have to look to see them, somewhere at the back of the picture?' says Livvy.

She does not ask him what is in his head and even if she did he is not sure he could say. She is an artist herself; that much he knows. She talks instead of drag and drop, set and pixels.

He offers her tea in a porcelain cup – an old Royal Worcester willow-pattern cup with a chipped rim and a handle so small it must have been made for a child, or perhaps women had smaller hands a hundred or more years ago. He saw Charlotte Brontë's dress once, on display in Haworth. She was small like a child and maybe she could have held the willow-pattern cup by its handle.

And he cuts Livvy a slice of banana bread, lifts it onto a small matching Royal Worcester tea-plate.

'Tell me a story from your life,' he says, 'and I'll tell you one from mine.'

*

'What would you do for love?' she says.

He shrugs, understanding that the question does not need his answer.

'I once was in love,' she says, 'with a boy who was as pretty as any girl and his breath was peppermint fresh and he said he loved me. Sounds like a story even as I say it. He was ten and I was eleven. It is the difference of only a year but every difference at that age is magnified so it felt like the difference of ten years and his kisses tasted illicit and like some sort of drug.

'"And what would you do for me?" he said, that peppermint-kiss boy, which is the same as saying, "What would you do for love?"

'"I'd walk on the breathless moon," I said.

'It was the middle of the day and there was no moon to test me with. Besides, it had already been done.

'"I'd dive to the bottom of the sea and bring up pearls to hang in your ears."

'And we were far from the sea and the boy thought pearls in his ears were too "girlie".

'"Would you put your arm in a hive of bees to fetch me some honey?" he said.

'"If you like," I said. And I put my hand in a hive of bees and stole a broken piece of honeycomb for love.'

'Did you not get stung?' said the old artist.

'I sang to the bees first, singing soft as breath, and I moved like moon-walk men move, which is slow and gentle, and my arm – the one I reached into the hive – I covered it first in shop-bought honey and like that the bees did not think me a threat, even as I broke their honeycomb.'

The old artist laughed.

'Maybe I misremember,' Livvy said. 'Maybe I make things up knowing how you wanted a story. I'd certainly make up a honeybee story for love.'

And just maybe she hadn't said that at all, not any of it. Maybe it was the old artist who had made up the honeybee story; he wasn't sure.

*

He clears his throat. The words are sticky at first and don't sound like his words at all.

'OK, so we are making up stories. Well, it is beyond sense, I know, but I believe in angels. I always have. William Blake once saw a tree all lit up and on every branch sat an angel in glory. And I think angels – invisible to all but the visionaries – guide our lives.

'I was in Venice once – have been there many times, and this was many years ago. And I wanted to be lost and away from the crowds. I tore up my map into a hundred pieces and dropped the pieces into a bin that smelled of fish and salt and lemons. I set my back to St Mark's Square and just walked.

'Into an area of yellow crumbling brick and empty squares where lace curtains hung at every open window and somewhere a woman was singing – her voice a little flat and off-key but dancing all the same – yes, voices can dance. The air was baked and I found it an effort to breathe.

'The canals were narrower here and not so pretty and the bridges had no walls or rails but were stone steps thrown crooked from one side to the other.

'I searched for shade but it was the middle of the day and the sun was directly above me.

'Then I heard the sound of hammer and chisel and somewhere a man was at work and there was a music to that work, as much as there had been in the woman singing. I spotted a workshop with its doors thrown wide. I knocked and entered.

'Inside was an old man – old as stone and quizzing glasses and clay pipes. He fetched me some water in a bowl that he first emptied of old nails and screws with broken threads. He wiped the bowl with his shirt tail and drew water from a small pump in the corner of his workshop.

'The water was so cold it left my lips numb – kisses never left my lips so numb.

'I nodded to thank him. No words were in my mouth, and even had there been I do not think he would have understood. He gestured for me to sit in a low armchair that had seen better days, and then picked up his hammer and chisel and continued with his work. He was a wood carver.

'The air in the workshop smelled of varnish and wax and the shavings of wood – which is the smell of hamster cages and mouse nests. And somewhere it also smelled of patchouli. That's important. Do you know what the smell of patchouli is?'

She understands the question does not need her answer and so she remains quiet and listening.

'I did not at first look at what he was carving. I was distracted by the smell of patchouli. There'd been a girl, you see. I sat down beside her in a gallery, so close I could have reached out and held her hand – sometimes when I tell the story I do just that. And she smelled of patchouli and I was a little bewitched by her. When she got up to leave I felt a part of me going with her.

'Once she had gone and I was alone again, and thinking I was eternally alone, I put one hand in my pocket and found a scrap of paper with a girl's name scribbled on it and her telephone number. I guessed it was *her* name and *her* number, but I left for Venice the next day and so thought I had missed my chance.

'And so the smell of patchouli there in the workshop – well, it surely meant something.

'I finished the water and put the empty bowl down on the floor beside the armchair. I found my voice and thanked the man. He looked up from his work and he said something, said it over and over so that I had it committed to memory before I left – "*Chiamala, chiamala.*"

'I did not know what he meant. When I got back to my hotel I asked the clerk at the desk if he could translate for me.

'He leaned across the desk and said in a whisper, "Call her. It means *call her.*"

'You see, the old man was an angel – he must have been, for that girl is now my wife.'

'It is a nice story,' Livvy says, but it is clear she does not really believe him.

*

'There should be an angel in this third picture, something hopeful and not of this world, but I am not sure yet. Maybe that is what the blurred man is looking up at. Maybe the angel will be more there in the next picture.'

The Fourth Picture

He'd said he believed in angels. She'd nodded and showed no surprise at his declaration. The old artist laughs at that. Maybe she understood it was just part of the story he told and had no other meaning beyond that.

'Did you think then of Botticelli's angels or Giotto's with their neat frescoed feathered wings in rainbow colours – like the green parakeets out of place in London's parks?'

Livvy laughs. He is sure she does. But then maybe this, all of it, is just a story he tells himself. His thinking is a little foggy. The doctor tests his blood and says he has an iron deficiency. It can happen at his age and with all he has gone through. He has to take a supplement. It upsets his stomach and turns his shit black. It is not easy to believe in angels on days like that.

'I am not sure what the next picture should be,' he tells her.

*

The doctor has also encouraged him to eat liver once a week and, thinking about that, he is reminded of a red-faced, pock-skinned maths teacher he once had. The old artist had a head for maths when he was a boy, that's what the teacher said. The answers to maths puzzles just came to him. But the teacher said he had to show his thinking. It is a beautiful feature of the subject that all mathematical thought can be shown – there's a schema for that. It is not so easy to show the thinking behind a work of art.

Livvy keeps to their arranged appointments. He does not. Some days he remains in bed with the curtains closed, feigning sleep, and his wife must answer the door and explain to Livvy that he is sick today. He can hear them talking in his studio then, not the words but the music of their talking.

'Do you know that there is no place for time in mathematics? Maths is out of time and in the end maybe there is just no place for time and time is simply an illusion we cling to.'

The old artist talks to himself some days and if that was written down it would be like showing his thinking.

'A man came up to me in the street once. Oh, years back it was, when I was young. He had a pack of playing cards in one hand and the sleeves of his jacket were rolled up to his elbows. He shuffled the cards so I could see they were just cards and all different. Then he cut them and folded them into each other and shuffled them again; then he fashioned them into a fan and he asked me to pick one. "Queen of Hearts," he said, even before I'd looked at the card. He did the trick three times and each time it was the Queen of Hearts that I picked. He winked at me and said that young men are all the same and young men are easy – always the Queen of Hearts, he said.'

*

Livvy is by his bedside one day. She holds his hand tight in hers – mothers hold hard to their children's hands just the same, just before crossing a busy road or a high bridge. It is quiet in the room, not even the sound of his breath or hers, and lying like that he thinks maybe he is already dead.

'I told the story of the angel wrong, I think.'

She nods. 'No more wrong than my story of the bees.'

'My father died – oh, years back now – and when I think of that old wood carver in Venice he has the face of my father. And when he offered me the armchair to sit in, I had something in my hand. I had the scrap of paper the girl in the gallery had put in my pocket, the paper with her name and telephone number on. I was reading what she had written, reading it over and over as though committing it to memory. That's when the old wood carver said I should call her – that's how he knew.'

When the old artist looks up she is gone from beside his bed – as if she had never been – and the room is empty.

*

Fathers do not speak easy with their grown children.

His wife reminds him to water the plants in the kitchen while she is out at work and to pay the window cleaner and to call his son. He nods but she is not sure he is really listening so she writes it down on a yellow Post-it and sticks the Post-it as a reminder on the door of his studio.

What is it about fathers and sons? he thinks. *Why is talk between them so hard? Is it just that they belong in different worlds and so speak in different languages?* Like the Venetian wood carver with his '*Chiamala,*' and the artist needing the young desk clerk to translate for him.

'I said before that I have been to Venice many times and each time I take myself off, away from the well-trodden path to the area of Santa Croce where I remember the red and yellow brick walls and the air hot as ovens and an old wood carver in a workshop with his doors thrown wide. But I never do find the place again, even when I think I have located the square,' he tells Livvy.

They are leafing through photographs of empty spaces – court-yards and squares and rooms with high ceilings or no ceilings at all.

One picture catches her eye. It shows a carrier bag hanging in a blue sky. She holds it up for him to see.

He shrugs with no answer.

*

He has more colour in his face one day and the curtains on all the windows are thrown wide and there is a new clarity to the day and to his thinking.

'I don't have it all worked out,' he says.

He's talking with his wife but for a moment he thought she was Livvy.

'You don't have to have it all worked out,' his wife says. 'It is not like maths. It's a little more mysterious than that.'

She is right of course and he knows that.

'In an empty space in Santa Croce one day – if ever a space can really be empty... it was at the hottest part of the day and there were no shadows to hide in and the windows on all the houses were open, like gaping mouths gasping for breath, and everywhere there was washing drying in the rippled blue air and everything still. I noticed a bird in a hanging cage; there was a cloth draped over the top of the cage so the bird was not in sunlight. It cocked its green head and looked up at me with a wet black eye.'

His wife says not a word.

'And suddenly there was something adrift – high up like clouds. It was a carrier bag but at first I thought it a sprite or an angel. In Venice it is easy to think a thing fanciful. It dropped – if dropping can be not like a stone – down into the empty square and seemed to fill it. I took a picture of it. An empty carrier bag in an empty sky above an empty square in Santa Croce.'

'*Chiamala*,' his wife says.

*

Livvy is taking notes.

'It's like something mathematical. Like showing my working out, my thinking.'

He has printed out a picture of an empty space, a pillared courtyard. There is a well in the centre of the picture and maybe it was the reason he took the picture in the first place. He wonders if that can be removed.

Livvy looks up and nods.

'And sky – I want there to be sky, so the upper floor should be removed and something like a wind-lifted carrier bag falling down on the square. Maybe a sheet.'

'Like an angel,' she said.

'I'm not sure,' he said.

'No?'

'Yes. That is to say, like an angel but also not. I am not sure that today I believe in angels.'

*

Sometimes there are no words. They sit in a quiet that is not quite silent. She drinks tea from a porcelain cup with a blue pattern on the bowl and a handle that is too small for her long fingers. And there is a chip on the rim that she avoids sometimes and at other times puts her tongue to, licking against the asperous surface of the chip.

Sometimes there is only thought.

*

It is not a complete thought, he admits that, and so not a complete picture. It has space in it, which, he thinks, all good thoughts do. And it is out of place and out of time also. He is both in the close-walled square and in the wide-open space of the Turbine Hall of Tate Modern; from the photograph of him and his wife, Livvy has set them neatly into the new space. He is wearing a dark coat, buttoned chin to knee, and a scarf, and he stands back on his heels. His wife stands beside him, holding on to his arm. She wears a long fur coat, bear or beaver or squirrel. And she looks out of the picture. By now we recognise them.

And a masked Punchinello is there: Livvy has put him half hidden behind one of the pillars, his arms folded as if he is waiting for something more – waiting for a crowd to spill into the picture. And Livvy is there too – pushed to one side and far back; she is quiet and she is looking too.

And falling down from a blue and thin-clouded sky is a white sheet, only in the light it is also blue, like a piece of the sky, like something Yves Klein might have done. Like something hopeful.

Hush.

'Not exactly an angel,' he says in a whisper so small it has no sound at all. 'Just the thought of an angel.'

*

Maybe maths is like that sometimes, is like a journey without a map and the mathematician just following a thread and not knowing where it will lead but trusting that it will lead somewhere.

*

I forgot to say that there is a dog in the picture, too – not a whippet or a greyhound but something with more hair, its tail like an old brush sweeping the stone-flagged square, or not sweeping it, for its tail is still and caught, and it sits on its haunches looking up at Punchinello as if eagerly expecting a biscuit or a bone or a trick.

The Fifth Picture

He likes things to be in their place. There's a comfort in that, in knowing that in the top drawer in the unit on his side of the bed is a pair of nail clippers he bought in a shop in Prague. Or the Bryant and May box of Swan Vestas safety matches to light the fire; they are kept behind the books on the middle shelf of the bookcase in the front room. Or the small key to the boiler cupboard, which hangs on a hook on the side of the fridge.

'Where's my blue woollen hat?'

'Your what?' says his wife.

He coughs, his fist to his mouth so that he catches that cough and holds it hot in his hand. 'Blueish-grey,' he says. 'It should be here, on the last of the coat hooks in the hall.'

'Yes, if we're back in 1983!'

Some things are so familiar that you expect them to be there even when they are not and cannot be. The blue hat had been eaten into holes by moths. But he is sure that he has seen it hanging on that last hook in the hall as recently as a week ago.

(This is not, as you might suppose in one so far on in years, a failure of memory. It is something else altogether.)

*

'Have you ever been to Paris?'

He holds a picture up for Livvy to see. Livvy with her blue eyes and the sun in her hair even on a cloudy day. He points to the shop in the picture.

'It is a famous bookshop. I think it is still there. I expect it is.'

'Shakespeare and Company?' She reads the name from the green sign hanging above the shop.

'Of course, it will be different now – it will smell different and taste different and the girl at the till will be a different girl.' There is something like exasperation in his words when he speaks them. He is, after all, a man who likes things to be just where he left them.

In the picture and in front of the shop is a woman dressed all in white with her hair pretty and a veil pinned to the back of her head. Another woman is beside her, dressed in red-coat and blue-jean ordinary, and fussing over the folds of the white dress; the plain girl is there to make sure the bride looks pretty. They have their backs to the camera.

'Out of the picture is a van where the Chinese bride changed into her dress. Apparently it is something they do in China. They have wedding pictures taken in places that are not part of the wedding. The shop had some meaning for the woman who was about to be married. I think the prospective groom was changing into his suit inside the van.'

'So it is as if they are married even before they are.'

'Yes, I like that. As though they have always been and so always will be. Like something blue and something eternal.'

He looks at Livvy and sees that she is without her cup of tea, the blue-and-white porcelain willow-pattern cup with the chip in the rim. He looks past her to his desk, to the arm of the chair in the corner and the small table piled high with books, but the cup is nowhere to be seen.

*

The other morning, so early that he was not really sure it could be called morning, he turned over in his bed and reached one arm out to his wife. But she was not there.

*

'In the picture there is something I did not notice before, not when I was taking it or when I much later printed it out. On the left-hand side is a young man – I call him the bachelor. He has a blue rucksack hoisted onto his back so that he leans a little forward, bearing the weight of the rucksack on the hunch of his shoulders. He is wearing a fringed scarf and a short grey jacket with buttons on the sleeve cuffs and a blueish-grey woollen hat that looks somehow familiar.'

Livvy thinks it might be a picture of the artist himself, as a boy... the boy if he had not followed the advice of the wood carver in Santa Croce, if he had not made the call.

'I should like the bachelor included in the new picture, and the Chinese bride, but pushed further back. And the girl tending the bride, can we change the colour of her coat so she does not draw the eye?'

He wants them all in the same space as the previous photograph, the empty courtyard with the arches and pillars, but he wants the upper floor put back in its place so there is no sky except what is reflected in the tall astragal windows.

'And you and your wife?'

He waves his hand in the air as though he is chasing off bees or wasps or moths.

'We will be there even when we are not,' he says.

*

He called out her name, his wife's name, sent it into the waking half-darkness of the not-yet-bright morning – not really like a summons but something nearer to prayer.

*

'And there is a fresco by Giandomenico Tiepolo. It is also in Ca' Rezzonico. It is of Punchinello in love – I may have mentioned it before. Punchinello is with a girl and they are dancing and he reaches one hand across to press the girl's breast. She does not seem to mind this groping of her body, though she too wears a mask so maybe she does mind and we do not see that she does. She carries a crown of flowers in one hand – maybe there is some meaning in her not wearing the crown, I don't know. I do not think it looks like love – not in Punchinello or in the girl – but I should like to include it in the picture, should like them half hidden behind one of the pillars.'

He sees that Livvy now has her cup of tea. It feels like a trick. Now you see it, now you don't. It occurs to him then that love can be a bit like that.

*

He got out of bed and put on the light, confirming that his wife was not there where she always was when he woke in the night.

*

'And exiting the courtyard – which must lead off into another courtyard exactly the same as the one they are leaving, as though it is something in a dream – a couple with their arms stretched across each other's backs. Lovers.'

He hands her a picture of the lovers he has recently taken.

Livvy nods and makes a note of what he wants in her small black book.

'And a monkey – maybe up high and between the two levels of the building. Here,' and he points to a space on the picture. 'Alone and sad like the bachelor who never gets the girl.'

*

'There you are,' he says. ('And not where you should be,' is what he does not say.)

His wife is in the studio. She has opened the curtains and light from the window spills silver and shiny into the room. She is looking at his work, her head bent over a picture he has printed off. Seeing her this way, the old artist thinks she looks like something painted by Vermeer.

'Monkeys are sometimes symbols for lust,' she says.

'It is from a painting by Giandomenico Tiepolo,' he says.

'It looks sad. Do you not think it looks sad? And the boy with the rucksack looks sad too.'

He nods.

'Is this one about love? Because I do not think it's complete. I think love can be more than this.'

He wants to tell her about how, when this picture is put next to the previous ones, there is an expectation created, an expectation of the old artist and his wife being there somewhere. He wants to say that their being there (even when they are not) is about love. And angels working their miracles unseen is about love, too. Hidden, maybe, but there all the same – even when they cannot be seen. Like his blueish-grey hat that will always have a place on the last coat hook on the wall beside the front door in the hall.

He does not say that the same is true for Livvy – that she is there too, out of sight but not out of mind. He does not say this, but maybe his wife knows.

He takes his wife's hand and leads her back to bed.

*

One side effect of the chemotherapy is a loss of libido and difficulty in gaining an erection. He is not to worry. This is perfectly normal and the doctors have all said that when the treatment is over, it is expected that at some point he will likely regain normal function. If not then there are pills that can help – blue pills. Not eternally blue but something more temporary.

The Sixth Picture

'It's something and nothing.'

Her silence interrogates him.

'Not what you think.'

That's a trap, telling her what she thinks.

'She's my hands,' he says.

The artist's wife nods as if this is a satisfactory answer to a question she has not asked.

*

When Livvy turns up the old artist says she is not to take off her coat. Then he thinks maybe they should have tea and cake first. He normally greets her with tea in a Royal Worcester blue willow-pattern cup and cake on a matching porcelain plate. It has become part of their time together.

'I want to go out today,' he says.

Maybe she thinks he wants to take some photographs. They have done that sometimes. Usually after tea and cake and some discussion of what pictures he wants and a route planned out.

'Where to?' she says.

He does not answer but merely waves one hand in the air as though questions could be spun like pink sugar on a stick, all threaded air and no substance.

He checks the camera is in his coat pocket.

She reminds him to pick up his walking stick before they leave the apartment.

*

They take the Tube into the centre of the city – a small boy in drab-coloured clothes lets the old man have his seat – and then they catch a train south. He buys the tickets after withdrawing cash from a hole in the wall. He takes pictures in the train station and she thinks maybe that is why they are there.

'I want to see the sea,' he says. 'Just to check it is still there.'

He sits back in his seat – he has taken the window seat. He loosens his scarf and pulls it from his neck. Conjurors pull handkerchiefs from their sleeves with just the same flourish.

They order tea from the trolley, tea in plastic cups that crackle if held too tight, and a slice of fruit cake that breaks into dry crumbs in their hands. But it is no matter, for today he is lit up.

*

Brighton is the end of the line. She takes his arm – just as his wife does now when they are out – and they walk the long slow sliding slope down to the sea. There's salt and sting in the air and the roads are busy even though it is out of season. They stop outside a sandwich shop on the way and he gives her some money to buy a carrier-bag lunch.

The beach is not as he remembered it, is all running pebbles that slip under his feet so that walking on them is not unlike walking on ice. And the sea – wasn't it blue once? He laughs.

They find a place under the pier, out of the wind. Livvy holds his hand – he does not know when that happened or what it means or even if it is true.

He asks her to take a picture and shows her what he wants.

*

'Where do you get your ideas from?'

'How would you define the work?'

'What does it all mean?'

It's not that he fears the questions. He wants them to be asked. That's part of the point. It's the answers that he frets over. He has come to a time in his life where the answers are like Brighton's running pebbles under his feet.

Questions are never wrong but answers can be wrong in so many ways. That's what he thinks.

He read something somewhere and he liked it, wrote it down – with a sharp new quill – and writes it again and again in idle moments, on the backs of old train tickets or folded into napkins or on the long blank edge of five-pound notes. He once wrote it on the door of a public toilet and he does not know why he did that. It is in French, maybe something by Maurice Blanchot, or a translation from the Latin sayings of Publilius Syrus; he forgets the context now.

'*Toute question ne mérite pas réponse.*'

He trots it out whenever someone asks him a question he does not care to answer.

'Not every question deserves an answer.'

*

He is tired on the journey back and sleeps. Livvy pats his arm and smiles. She does not know what today has been about but she has learned to be patient and not to ask questions.

When the conductor comes to check their tickets she does not wake him, reaches with the nip of finger and thumb into his coat pocket for his ticket and sees he has written something in French on the back – she does not know when he did that. The conductor mouths the words to himself, and with his schoolboy French is not able to understand what the old artist has written. The conductor clips the ticket and passes it back to Livvy.

*

Anywhere. The destination is not the point. The journey is the point. They are at an airport desk, passports in hand and the woman behind the desk is asking where it is they want to go.

'Anywhere, somewhere, nowhere,' he says.

'Is that like saying "you choose"?' his wife says.

The sound of suitcases on wheels trundling over the hard floor of the airport makes a small thunder. It is a warning of rain. He waves one hand in the air like a conjuror when he flicks a handkerchief and suddenly it is a wing-flapping dove or a bouquet of flowers.

'I must have a destination,' says the woman behind the desk. She looks familiar – wears a feathered hat and a hook-nosed face mask and a crown of flowers.

It is all just a dream, he knows that on some level, and so the question of a destination is not important. Maybe in the dream he says that – thoughts in dreams are sometimes the same as things said.

'A ticket to somewhere and nowhere,' he says.

Punchinello stands behind the woman at the airport desk. He reaches one hand round and lays it on her cloth-covered breast, presses his fingers into the dress, into her flesh.

*

Livvy has to wake him when they reach London.

'You missed the journey,' she says.

He laughs.

They take a few photographs in the station – passengers going somewhere and nowhere, their faces anxious and expectant, the wheels of their suitcases dragging noisily over the grey station floor.

'It has been a good day, I think,' he says.

Livvy nods.

'Not our usual day,' she says.

'Exactly.'

*

He sends Livvy home in a taxi, gives her money for the fare. They will meet again in a week and they can look over the photographs then.

'I have an idea for the next picture,' he says.

*

'To Brighton with Livvy,' he says. 'It's something and nothing.'

Her silence interrogates him.

'Not what you think.'

That's a trap, telling her what she thinks.

'She's my hands.'

The artist's wife nods as if this is a satisfactory answer to a question she has not asked.

He waves one hand in the air, stirs it – but it is not this time like spun sugar but like three-day-old soup.

'Ask me anything you like, anything at all,' he says.

*

A week later the artist, with Livvy's help, makes his sixth picture in the series. It's part of the journey, is all he says, and she thinks he is making a joke.

He serves her tea in a chipped blue porcelain cup and cake on a matching blue plate. His hand shakes as he passes her the cake. Maybe she does not notice.

The sixth picture comes easier than the others. He has thought about it a lot since their last meeting.

'Sometimes the pictures, even when they are just thoughts in my head, have all the physical reality of a room and I can walk about in them and sleep in them and talk to the walls.'

There are rough sketches on his desk, maybe a dozen of them – showing his working out if this were maths. Nothing is finished in the drawings, for he still has difficulty holding a pencil for any time.

In the picture they work on there are passengers pulling suit-cases on wheels, looking all ways and looking lost – no, not lost exactly but knotted together and looking as if they are going somewhere and nowhere both at the same time. Maybe they are not going but coming and the picture is one of arrival. It is a question he knows will be asked. And one of Giandomenico Tiepolo's painted ladies is there too, wearing a red floppy hat, with pearl earrings and a pearl necklace and a dress cut so low at the front you can see something of the boast of her breasts; and Punchinello is hiding in the picture too – smirking no doubt, though his white conical hat is all there is to see. And right at the back, reflected in a mirrored or glass wall, are the artist and his wife.

'They *must* be in the picture,' he says.

Livvy does not ask why he refers to himself and his wife as 'they', does not ask why 'they' *must* be in the picture, does not remark on her own absence or the absence of angels. She makes some notes in her book, sets these aside and sips at her tea, the bowl of the cup cradled in her hand as though she is holding a new-laid egg.

He notices the handle of the cup; it is a neat and perfect porcelain ring, like something that could be easily slipped onto a girl's finger. He does not know why he has not had that thought before, why he has it now.

Is there a question here?

He feels a little unsteady on his feet, like walking again on Brighton's running pebbles – he reaches for Livvy's hand to steady himself.

Not every question deserves an answer.

She's my hands, he thinks, and maybe things thought are the same as things said, even when they are not the stuff of dreams. And maybe a thing can be true and not true at one and the same time.

The Seventh Picture

'Perhaps you can tell me what it is. Why girls look so longingly into their mobile phones. It is like a new sense through which they experience the new world, or they miss experience with so much looking. I don't understand. They seem to be searching for something, their fingers turning pages and pages of books, like there is a line they have lost that will give them meaning or hope or love.'

The old artist has taken a photograph of two teenage girls, sitting on a step in the station. Their bags are at their feet and though they do not talk to each other it is clear they are together. One of the girls looks off out of the picture, one hand cupped like she holds breadcrumbs and waits only for birds to feed; the other girl stares down at her phone. One is casting her gaze like a net or like sowing seed; the other is focused, holds her phone up to her face, peers into the screen. Maybe she is anxious.

'I think it is something like love,' Livvy says. 'But there are many kinds of love.'

*

Livvy had settled him onto a bench in the station, fussed over his scarf and his stick, then gone to find out the time of the next train to Brighton. She was gone for longer than he thought it would take and he missed her, felt suddenly how alone he was in the busy station. Maybe it was his wife he missed, then. He looked up and saw Livvy from a distance and he knew she did not feel watched. She had her hair loose and she took one finger and caught a wisp of her hair and tucked it behind one ear. He snatched for breath, tucked the memory of that moment into his waistcoat pocket.

*

Does a husband ever believe that he knows his wife, really knows her? What she thinks, what she feels? Knows her from the small scolds she throws after him when he does something wrong or the soft spoken endearments she gifts him when she remembers that she loves him or loved him once?

Sometimes, it is true, a wife thinks she knows her husband, even though he is taciturn and keeps his thoughts wrapped up like doves in conjuror's cloths and only sets them free when he is sure he is not watched or when he has practised the trick enough for it to be easy. (No doves have been harmed in the performance of his thoughts.)

And the old artist's pictures? Perhaps that is why he refuses to define his work or to explain. That is something he might so easily get wrong. Perhaps also he does not fully see all the thoughts he has put into his pictures; that's how art works sometimes and is not at all like maths. Besides it might just as well be that no man (or woman) fully knows himself. Even a good man. That is, when all's said and done, part of the journey.

*

'You do something with your hair. I want to catch that and to put it into the next picture in the series. And girls looking into their phones right at the centre. And a boy in drab-coloured clothes, like the boy on the tube who got up to give me his seat. It feels important somehow.'

She looks at him funny.

He blushes but he does not know that he does.

He mimes the thing she does, one finger catching his hair if his hair was long, and dragging it behind one ear. Just one finger, like gently stroking her brow.

She laughs. 'Just that?' she says. 'It's something most girls do and some boys do it, too.'

He shrugs and says he cannot explain.

What he does not say is that it is something his wife does sometimes when her hair is not pinned up from her face, something he saw her do when she was just a girl sitting on a bench in a gallery staring into the blue – looking for meaning or hope or love. It was what caught his eye and he snatched for breath then and sat down beside her wanting to put into words what he had just seen her do, for he knew she had done it unawares, as Livvy had; unaware of how small but how exquisitely beautiful a thing it was.

'Like this,' she says and she does it for him.

'Yes,' he says, 'but far off and not as though you are seen.'

Maybe it is not so beautiful when given as a performance but must be something done unawares. Or it must be something illicit and stolen.

*

She never checks her phone when she is with him.

'It's about colour and composition and shape,' the old artist says.

It is two weeks after the Brighton trip and he is explaining what he wants for the next picture. He approaches it as though it is a painting and when he sees what she does on the computer screen, he asks if she can shift things about a bit. There's a small boy caught at the very front of the picture, so close to the viewer that he is out of focus. He is dressed all in blue. And in the mirror – or maybe it is a distorted glass wall – at the back of the picture, the same boy, the same picture of him, only smaller and Livvy has altered the blue to a poppy red just as he had instructed. The boy seen twice like that in two places at once – in two worlds at once – is like a ghost, as though he does not really exist, and to the girl with her head bent over her phone he doesn't.

'But what about the boy in drab clothes?' she says.

It was a thought in his head. He must have told her about him.

'I do not see any photographs of him.'

'No,' he says. 'There are no photographs of him but I have an idea.'

He consults a book from the shelves that line one wall of his studio, art books mostly. He does it almost without thinking, like it is a trick he has practised so well that he can do it without really attending to what he is doing. He flicks through the pages – like a girl flicking through the pages on her phone – until he finds what he is looking for.

'There,' he says.

Livvy does not see him at first, the boy. It is a picture in bright colours. It is by the artist Jacopo da Pontormo, a biblical scene: *Joseph with Jacob in Egypt*. There are levels to the picture and stairs leading down and leading up. On one of the steps sits a boy who is a little out of place, who belongs not in Joseph's time but to Pontormo's time. He is dressed in drab-coloured clothes and sits beside a brown bag as though he has been shopping for cabbages and carrots, and fish wrapped in paper or cloth. The story is told that the boy was apprenticed to the artist, though why Pontormo chose to put the boy into his picture is not clear. The boy grew up to be the artist Bronzino and in the National Gallery in London hangs his best-known work, *An Allegory with Venus and Cupid*. An erotically charged picture, it is also in some way about love.

'Can we lift the boy from the steps in Pontormo's picture and put him reflected in the mirror or behind the glass wall so that he is of the world that is not in this world?'

He has arranged that the picture of Livvy tucking her hair behind her ear is also in this other world. He wishes that he had a picture of his wife doing that thing with her hair – not his wife as she is now, but as she was when he first saw her and she did not know him but still wanted so much to see him again, wanting it so much that she left her name and her number in his pocket.

*

There's a falling cloth in this latest picture too, the same cloth that falls in some of the other pictures, but in this picture it can easily be missed, for it is not fully there but half in the frame and half out, now you see it now you don't. It is like a conjuror's outsized white handkerchief that is lifted with a flourish to reveal the trick underneath, or like a tablecloth that is pulled from the set table and everything that was sitting on the white spread cloth is left in place on the table and nothing falls to the floor or breaks; and in the picture the white cloth is falling or suspended in the air high above the boy in drab clothes and Livvy tucking her hair behind her ear and the girl looking for meaning and hope and love on her phone.

This must not be understood as an explanation of the cloth, for sometimes it might be thought of as an angel – no one says that an angel must be feathered like a bird or have the shape and form of a man or a woman. Sometimes an angel can be just a thought or an idea – like love.

*

It is true what Livvy said, that there are many kinds of love, but I think people forget that and roll all love into a ball and call it one thing. The thing she did with her hair – and the old artist is thinking about his wife now and not about Livvy – and how he felt when he saw her do that, somehow there was meaning and hope and love in that. The old artist does not tell anyone this, not even his wife, but maybe she knows.

The Eighth Picture

He talks to himself when he's alone, tells his wife it is only thinking out loud, but does not say to her about the lucent shimmering air in one corner of his studio. Like heat rising from a hot road and the whole world ripples as though it is drowned and underwater.

'It will happen,' the old artist says, and he's talking now about Venice and how the sea will someday take back what is hers, and standing just out of view Giandomenico Tiepolo weeps and the old artist looks again at a picture of the fresco, *Il Mondo Nuovo*, and he sees then that Giandomenico Tiepolo does not lift a monocle to his eye as he'd first thought but it is a cloth in his hand and maybe Giandomenico Tiepolo understands what the old artist is saying out loud, what he says about Venice being one day returned to the sea, and Giandomenico Tiepolo dries away his tears.

*

He loses things too, is always looking under tables and behind chairs. Maybe things missing are not lost but merely hidden. Like the blue-grey woollen hat, and one day it was moth-eaten and the holes became one hole and the hat slipped out of this world into the world of his imagination and the bachelor with the rucksack on his back wears it now.

He loses keys – don't we all do that – and shoes and cups. And names he loses also, not only the names of people but of things. Suddenly and in the middle of sentences, just when he is sure that he knows and he does not expect to have lost anything, and then he stumbles and he does not know what the thing for boiling water is called.

'Not a teapot, but the thing before,' he says, and he is talking to himself again or to the bright shaken air so no one notices the lost name or the brief and momentary panic in the old artist when he understands it is lost.

He thinks it is as though the whole world – his world (is it an old world?) – is broken. Like seeing everything reflected in a mirror and the mirror cracked into a hundred shards or the mirror pocked and blemished so in places there is no reflection.

He forgets how to do things, too. Livvy ties his shoelaces for him some days or he wears his shoes untied and the laces tucked in under his sock so he walks as though he is dancing or treading barefoot over sharp stones. He forgets where things that should be familiar are located, searches all the kitchen drawers for teaspoons or butter knives and he should know where they are without looking or thinking.

And always just out of sight he thinks he sees something – like a carrier bag lifted on the air outside his window or a piece of paper caught in a draught or a cloth that floats like a torn kite above the fireplace. He thinks maybe there are angels gathering. It is the end of summer and maybe he mistakes birds for angels.

*

'How are you today?' says the doctor.

He says he is a little stiff and he says maybe that is the fault of age and not moving as much as he should. He doesn't say that he does not leave the house some days because he cannot find his shoes or his walking stick. Or is so stiff he cannot reach down to put on his socks and walks un-socked through the apartment looking for teaspoons.

The doctor carries out more tests. He smiles and says they are routine, but the old artist is not so sure. He sees Giandomenico Tiepolo weeping again, looks up to the ceiling and sees a ripple in the air and thinks maybe there was an angel there briefly.

'You should get out more,' the doctor says. 'Not just sitting at your desk or easel all day.' (The doctor has a limited understanding of what the artist does when he is working.) 'The air is good for you, a walk every day.'

The artist says he went to Brighton for the day with Livvy, walked hand in hand on the slip-sliding beach and the salted air stung and he saw a girl tuck a whisper of hair behind one ear and it was the perfect moment. But when pressed he does not remember when any of that was, thinks maybe it was something he did a long time ago or only in his imagination.

'It is about balance,' says the doctor.

This is exactly what his wife has been saying to him for weeks now. 'Take a breath.'

He swallows air and holds it. The doctor listens to his heart – at least that's what the artist thinks and he is worried that the doctor will hear something that the artist keeps hidden.

'Do hearts play a different tune when a man is in love?' he says, or maybe that is just a thought in his head, an imbalance of sorts.

The doctor says he can put on his shirt again.

'Yes,' he says to the old artist, 'it is always about balance.'

Balancing this world with the new world or the world in his head. Or Giandomenico Tiepolo's world. Balance is there in the pictures he makes – he hopes it is and he wants then to show the doctor his work, not to explain anything, for he would be sure to explain it wrong, but just so the doctor can make his own mind up.

*

'Maybe there should be more air in this picture,' Livvy says.

He considers this, then nods his approval. After all, hadn't the doctor said the air would do him good? Clear his head, maybe, though he is not sure he needs a clear head for the work he is doing.

'Yes, I see. So that the outside is somehow breaking into the picture. Like a door left open somewhere and you can see the light and there's an easy passage between the two worlds, the world of indoors and the world of outdoors.' But he also wants the picture to be somehow suffocating – like a whole city drowning.

She takes his photograph of the stairs in the Turbine Hall of Tate Modern, distorted a little in the mirrored wall so that it is not clear if the steps are an ascent or a descent, and she sets it at the back of the new picture and the light there is silvery. He says he likes that and he thinks if he could only walk into that light he'd find his lost keys and his blue-grey woollen hat before the moths got to it and teaspoons and the name for the thing that he boils water in to make tea.

Livvy lifts the blue willow-pattern porcelain cup to her lips, kisses the chipped rim and sips at the tea. He licks his own lips and he does not know that he does.

'I want only a glimpse of the falling cloth in this picture,' he says to Livvy – *like the angel is leaving the picture*, he thinks, though he does not say this out loud.

Later he will kiss his wife's lips and imagine her young again and doing that thing with her hair that Livvy does and that his wife did first – and he will tell his wife that he loves her, loves her in the old world and in the new. She will want to know what the doctor said, except he went without her knowing.

'Do you know I have been there, to Venice, when the water was so high there were gondolas adrift in St Mark's Square and duckboards laid down so that women in summer shoes or long dresses could cross from one coffee bar to the next and it was like seeing them walking on water?'

He does not at first know why he thought to tell Livvy this.

'And all of Venice rippled and the waves lap-lapping at the windows and licking just beneath the stone balconies of palaces that will one day sink into the mud. And church doors could not hold back the water so that fish smacked their lips looking up open-mouthed at stone-carved saints in ecstasy and anticipating kisses.'

Maybe Livvy writes these thoughts down in her black notebook.

'And this picture must have something of all of that, something of the drowned city and the old world lapping against the new world, and the people looking up, looking down, as though they have lost the names for things, or shoes they have lost or butter knives. And Giandomenico Tiepolo weeping – did you know he was weeping? And right in the centre something painted and something real, like two sides of a coin, something past and something present, a figure from this world and a figure from Tiepolo's and "How do you do?" they say to one another, and they bow to each other.

'And a breathlessness in the picture.'

'Take a breath,' said the doctor and he listened to the old artist's heart.

'And also in the picture somewhere, lost or hidden, the artist looking for a photograph to take – myself looking for a story to tell – and his wife, my wife, looking off out of the picture, looking for angels or birds or teaspoons.'

*

He read something somewhere about the true daughters of Venice and how they might be known. Like a test, like looking for the girl that danced so well at the ball and she left behind a glass slipper so small and so fine that there can only be one foot that the slipper fits. The daughters of Venice are pretty and few now but if you remove their shoes – so like the fairy tale – and their socks, it can be seen that they have webbed feet. That is how they are able to walk about the city when the water is everywhere.

Then the old artist looks again at Giandomenico's fresco, *Il Mondo Nuovo*, magnifies the picture through glass to better see the slumped shoulders of the lumpen women and the ladies in frilly dresses and feathered or mob caps, and he does not believe any of them can walk on water.

*

'The doctor said I should go out more. For the air and so my thoughts are not cloudy and so I do not lose walking sticks or woollen hats but lose only stiffness. He said nothing about angels or keys or kettles (see, I have found the name again). He slapped me on the back as though we were friends and said I have the heart of a much younger man and he said I have a lover's heart.'

The old artist is in his studio again, talking to himself, talking to the lucent shimmering air.

His wife pops her head round the studio door and is surprised to see him alone.

'Just thinking out loud,' he says.

'And the doctor?'

He thought he had kept it from her. He'd hidden the letter telling him of the appointment, tucked it down the back of the sofa where the lost pennies and paperclips go, had attended the hospital alone this time, wearing odd socks and shoes without laces. He thought his wife had been through enough already.

'Just routine. Nothing to worry about,' says the old artist.

'Nothing?' she says, looking past him and out of the picture. Looking to where the air is lucent and shimmering.

Giandomenico Tiepolo is weeping again, somewhere he is, and through the tears he makes answer for the old artist: 'Something and nothing is what it is. He thinks he has a lover's heart. It is a common ailment in a man so far on in years.'

Of course, the weeping Giandomenico Tiepolo is nothing more than a thought in the old artist's head, his lips making the spittle shape of the words spoken but holding back all sound of them, the quiet murmur of water running over stones.

The Ninth Picture

He has started dropping teaspoons. His grip on them loosens
and then he cannot keep hold. Pencils and plates, too. One day
he drops Livvy's blue porcelain tea cup and it breaks into a dozen
pieces that will not go back together again. He does not know if
there is meaning in that, in the dropping and the breaking and the
not going back together. His wife finds him sitting on the kitchen
floor gathering the pieces of the broken cup together into a nest of
cloth – a handkerchief or napkin. He weeps.

'It's just a cup,' his wife says. 'We are not short of cups.'

His wife bends to pick up the cloth nest he has made of the
broken cup and like that she looks familiar and he remembers the
bending woman in the last picture he made, the woman looking
for the lost names of things or shoes that are missing or dropped
butter knives.

*

Even more air. The inside bursting outside, barging through the
glass walls and onto a beach, a yellow sandy beach and not a
beach with pebbles. That is his idea for the next picture, but he
has mislaid his walking stick and cannot reach to put on his socks.

Instead, he has bought a bag of sand, had it delivered to the door. Too heavy for him to lift so he has the delivery man put it down in the hall. Then, a cupful at a time, he carries the sand into his studio, tips it over the floor. It takes him most of the morning. Then he throws the windows wide and he is undressed and his feet in the sand, the sand between his toes.

He has looked through his archive of photographs and found pictures of beaches whose names he has misplaced. He has pinned the pictures up on the walls of his studio.

Outside the sun is losing its heat and the light is silvery and birds have collected on the telephone wires. Summer-visiting swallows and swifts, and they have not the heart for our winters and all their chatter now is of new worlds to go to, long-hot-summer worlds.

The phone in the hall rings. He pretends not to hear it. Then a brief quiet followed somewhere by the ringing of his mobile phone. He does not make to answer this either.

*

He marks the days off on his calendar. Two more before Livvy is to visit. From his studio window he sees a bird at the feeder in the garden. Then two, then five. Squabbling with each other. Starlings, he thinks. Ugly and beautiful in equal measure, the sleek pugilists of the bird feeder, their feathers all oil-slick blue and rainbows.

'Do you know that the wings of angels were once more than white? Were all colours. Look at Giotto's angels: their wings are the wings of exotic birds, parrots in paradise. We must have starlings in the picture – a cloud of them.'

He thinks when they are gathered like that it is called a murmuration and the birds paint pictures in the air, or spaces they make, holes in a blue woollen cap, but then they shift again, the air seeming to ripple and closing the gaps again.

'It is something they do to confuse the birds that would attack them. Goshawks and merlins and peregrines. I heard that somewhere.'

He is talking to himself again. Thinking out loud. Practising what he will say to Livvy when she comes.

'I am sorry about the cup – your cup. I dropped it or it flew startled from my hands.'

The phone in the hall rings – the third time today it has done so. He feels a falcon threat. He waves one hand in the air, dismissively, as though the sound of the phone ringing can be chased off like shooing cats or chickens.

*

His wife catches him in the hall. He is walking a line, his arms out from his sides and all his concentration on not wavering, though he does. It's as though he walks a tightrope strung between the front door and the kitchen. Maybe she remembers him young and doing tricks to catch her eye. Leaping over walls to fetch flowers from garden plots; running up hills just so he could run back to her, breathless and excited; walking on the edges of pavements, a book on his head that does not fall.

She looks at him and her look is all questions.

'Balance,' he says.

The next morning, on the desk in his studio she has placed a book just where he will find it, marked a page in the book with a piece of paper and one word written on the paper.

It is a picture of acrobats, something from an old painting. Boat builders or seamen at play, he thinks, and they have made themselves into a human pyramid, so high that the man at the top might be touching the sky and the men on the levels below show the strain of holding the weight of the pyramid up and they waver, as though they might drop the men at the top, easy as dropping teaspoons or pencils or plates.

His wife has written the word 'balance' on the paper. He laughs and thinks he will put the clumsy acrobats into the next picture, with an upset murmuration of starlings and a masked bird of prey in anklets and jesses sitting patient on a fence post. Everything seen through a torn gap in a curtain of glass, the glass seeming to dissolve so soon there is nothing to differentiate here from there, the new world from the old, Giandomenico Tiepolo from the old artist. A collision of sorts, a dropping of the veil, a harrier among star-startled starlings, and a breathlessness then, which is something still and without sound and also is a panic.

The phone in the hall rings again.

*

He watches for her coming, sand between his toes and the windows wide again and starlings visiting the feeder in the garden.

Then Livvy is at the door and he asks her to remove her shoes. He has never done that before. He ushers her through to the beach in his studio and goes to fetch her tea in a new cup and cake on an old plate.

He does not tell her about dropping the blue porcelain cup and the pieces wrapped in cloth and hidden or lost in a desk drawer in his studio.

'The new picture?' she says with her feet in the sand and the window thrown open so the day outside is pulled inside.

He nods and looks pleased with himself.

'I had a window in my apartment open just the same,' she says, 'and a bird flew into my bedroom, threw itself in a panic against the walls and fell behind the bed. I knelt on the carpet and looked under the bed. I could see it curled into itself and panting for breath with its head canted to one side as though it was looking at me with the study of its black wet eye. I lay down on the floor, half under the bed and half not. I made soft watery noises, cooing like small doves, and like that the bird seemed after some time to settle.'

Telling the story, Livvy's voice has become small, like a whisper that must be tucked behind the ear.

'And time slipped away so the room was then dark – not shut-cupboards dark or deep-pockets dark, but streetlight-under-a-hedge dark. I took the cloth case from a pillow and caught the bird in its soft folds, could feel the panic rising again in its soft breast. I carried it to the open window and set it down on the sill. It was not there in the morning when I woke.'

'They say a bird in your house is like an angel looking out for you.'

The phone in the hall starts ringing.

He does not move.

'Do you want me to get that?' Livvy says.

*

'We are nearing the end of the journey,' the old artist tells Livvy.

'Yes,' she says. 'I had a feeling we were.'

He has arranged all the finished pictures on his desk and on his chair, in sequence, like they tell a story, like they can be read.

'There is still the most important picture to come, but all the ingredients are here.'

'It's just a case of putting them all together,' she says.

He asks her if she could help him on with his socks and his shoes.

She kneels and does as he asks, wipes the sand from the soles of his feet and between his toes, uses a white handkerchief that he takes from his pocket for the purpose.

'I am sorry about your cup,' he says under his breath, says it so quietly it has all the substance of a thing thought and nothing more than that.

*

When his wife returns from work he offers to make her a cup of tea and he clears a space for her at the kitchen table, holds the chair back for her to sit. She sits and watches him, looking for the faults in what he does: he walks with his stick today, looks in the wrong drawer for the teaspoons and forgets to put the milk into the cup first. They are all small things of no consequence.

'How was Livvy today?'

He nods, says she was good. Says they are almost finished.

She adds a little more milk to her tea and lifts the cup to her kissing-lips.

'The doctor at the hospital called this afternoon,' he says.

She sets the cup back down in its saucer.

He looks to the ceiling, looking for angels or kites or kestrels.

'Oh,' she says.

'He wants to see me again. Something about the tests he did. Something he needs to discuss with me face-to-face rather than over the phone.'

He holds his breath, feels the rising small panic of a bird when it is caught in pillowcase folds and a gentle girl is making dove calls to calm it.

His wife drops a teaspoon and it makes a harsh ringing sound as it hits the floor.

'I'd like it if you were there with me,' he says.

'Yes, of course,' she says.

The men in the human pyramid suffer an imbalance then and everything topples and some at the top are caught in the arms of other men and some tumble in the sand and there is more laughter than cursing.

'Of course,' she says again.

She reaches across the table and takes his hand in hers.

The Tenth Picture

'Heads you win, tails you lose,' he says.

'Win what?' Livvy says.

The old artist thought it would be enough to win or to not win. He hadn't thought of a prize.

'The last piece of cake,' he says, not sure that she hadn't already had the last piece.

'Well, that's something,' she says.

He shows her an old silver coin, flips it over so she can see the head of a pretty new Queen Elizabeth on one side and the coats of arms of the four nations on the tail side. He tosses it into the air, catches it with one hand and slaps it down on the back of his other hand.

It is an old half-crown. When he was a small child it had once filled the palm of his hand, bigger than old pennies and heavy. His grandmother had given it to him as a reward for going out to the ice-cream van in the street to buy her cigarettes – she'd written what she wanted down on a torn piece of newspaper and slipped a ten-bob note along with her order into a mean-clipped clasp purse that he was to give to the man serving cones from a glass window on the side of the van.

His grandmother died before he was ten.

'She is with the angels now,' his father had said.

She died from cancer and by then he understood that cigarettes could kill and so he felt guilty that he had played a part in her death when he'd bought her a pack of ten Black Cat cigarettes from a man who would have done better to just sell ice-cream. The half-crown in his hand was smaller by then but it felt so much heavier.

*

His wife has left him a note. *It will be OK*, she has written. He finds the note tucked into the pocket of his trousers late in the morning. It is a little crumpled by then and so he does not know if it is a new note or one that he has read before, does not know if it is the visit to the hospital that will be OK or some other smaller event.

*

He coughs – makes a small loose fist that he brings up to his mouth. Then, his voice all rasp and rust, he says they should make a start on the next picture.

'It is perhaps the most important one of them all. The one we have been working towards.'

He has pinned up on the studio wall a print of Giandomenico Tiepolo's *Il Mondo Nuovo*. He stands in front of the print and is a little breathless. The colours in the print are quite washed out and not at all as he remembers them. And the light in his studio has none of the lucent clarity of the light in Venice.

'I see it differently today from how I saw it yesterday. Yesterday I noticed the carnival more and today the heavy-set woman with the slumped shoulders catches my eye and Giandomenico Tiepolo weeping and all the attention of the crowd focused on the one thing.'

Livvy leans in a little, looking to see Giandomenico Tiepolo weeping.

'I thought, when we started out with our pictures, that I wanted to know what it was the crowd were all looking at in Giandomenico Tiepolo's fresco. I thought the picture asked as much of the viewer and that was our journey. A shift into the light where angels are.'

She comes up beside him in front of the print of the fresco. She takes his hand in hers.

He clears his throat; 'I thought that the artist in the picture held up a monocle or a quizzing glass to his hidden eye, but then I saw that it was a cloth in his hand and so I think he weeps.'

'It changes things,' she says.

'Changes everything,' he says.

*

'I am decided,' he says. 'I want this picture, our picture, to be the mirror of Giandomenico Tiepolo's fresco, as though we see the wide-angle shot of the crowd from the other side. Their faces in particular. And the crowd will be our crowd.'

'Heads and tails,' she says.

'Heads you win, tails you lose.'

He tosses his grandmother's half-crown into the air and catches it in the close of one hand.

When he thinks about the coin now, he is not sure it is the same half-crown that his grandmother gave him in reward for going to the ice-cream van for her Black Cat cigarettes. Surely he spent that half-crown – thirty pennies' worth of humbugs or fruit salad chews or toffee dainties? And this coin in his hand? He sees that it is dated 1953, the first year of the pretty Queen's reign. Something doesn't quite fit. Maybe it was a George VI half-crown he had from his grandmother and this Queen Elizabeth coin is something he later came by and he simply attached the old story to the new coin.

'It is like we are making a memory,' he says, 'as long as memory is understood as something artificial and shifting – like pebbles on a beach or sand. No, not creating something new, but taking a memory that has become dull and making it bright again, brighter than it ever was before.'

Livvy brings up a blank page on the computer screen.

'Actually, I am almost tempted to leave our picture blank and shiny,' he says then. 'There is almost enough in that, I think.'

*

Sometimes he feels acutely as though he is alone in the world. It is something he has always felt. Like the moment after the umbilical cord is cut and the baby is for the first time separate from the mother. And all this, all his life and his work, has been a search for connection or reconnection.

But then, isn't that the same for everyone?

*

His wife leaves her work early. She has arranged for a taxi to take them both to the hospital to keep his appointment. She left a note in one of his shoes to remind him of the time of his appointment.

He sits on a chair in the hall waiting for the sound of her feet on the stairs on the other side of the door, the sound of her key in the lock. He is dressed in his long coat and a scarf that Livvy wrapped about his neck before she left and he rests his hands on the curled head of his walking stick.

'Do you hear it?' he says.

He is alone and his words do not connect with anything or anyone.

*

He does not like the smell of the hospital or the way people talk in hushed voices as though they are in church or reading stones in a graveyard. He thinks of *Il Mondo Nuovo* and it occurs to him that even when he was in the Ca' Rezzonico gallery standing in front of Giandomenico Tiepolo's fresco, there was no sound from the picture and the whole crowd held its breath. An anticipation of something new and maybe the whole world new.

Outside, an ambulance brings the banshee-wail of its siren almost to the door of the hospital.

In the old artist's head he hears a bird screaming, feels the flap of its great wings about his head, sees the quick flash of its talons and a hundred flung-in-the-air angels flying all ways.

'It will be OK,' his wife says and she pats his arm and leads him to the right department.

'Heads you win, tails you lose,' he says under his breathless breath and his hand in his trouser pocket clutches at the half-crown that was bigger once and might or might not have been given to him by his grandmother.

*

Livvy has positioned him, according to the instructions, on the far left-hand side of the picture, in profile this time, the mirror of Giandomenico Tiepolo and his father. He holds his camera up looking into the screen on the back, looking for a story there somewhere. And his wife is beside him – should she not be on the other side? – and she is looking out of the picture. And one of three capped and masked Punchinello figures looks over his wife's shoulder, looking at what is on the screen on the back of the old artist's camera.

'Heads you win, tails you lose,' the masked Punchinello whispers.

*

The air in the doctor's room seems charged and heightened. The doctor asks the old artist and his wife to sit. There are two comfortable chairs arranged so that they are turned slightly into each other and both facing the doctor in his chair.

Does he look more serious than smile? Is there a waver in his voice? Does his hand shake as he shuffles through the papers in the old artist's file?

'It will be OK,' his wife does not say.

'Thank you for coming in today,' the doctor begins. 'I'll get right to it. Your tests show that the cancer that was in your left lung has cleared and not returned. But the bad news is that there is a new cancer and it is in your right lung. It is a more aggressive cancer than before and it has already spread beyond the lung and I am so sorry but there is nothing we can do.'

Heads you win, tails you lose.

*

He remembers something that Leonardo had written – maybe in one of his notebooks or in a letter to his lover or on the plastered wall of his bedroom. Leonardo considered 'nothing to be more certain than death and nothing more uncertain than the hour'.

The doctor could not say when. He said they should go away and spend time together and if there was anything they wanted to know they could call him.

*

There was once a paperback bookshop in Edinburgh, so far back in memory that he has forgotten its name. And a woman there – a proper and good-mannered Edinburgh lady – did not like one of the books on the shelves and she bought a copy and took it outside, holding it between the pinch of finger and thumb as though it was something dirty or obscene. She poured petrol over the book and set it alight.

He has a memory of the shop and still has some of the books he bought there. But he is not certain about the lady burning the book. It was talked about in the bars where he drank and they laughed at the woman's name and they called her silly and stupid and cunt. He has seen black-and-white pictures of the lady and the book all aflame, pictures that were printed in the newspapers and everything spins and he thinks that the memory he has of that burning-book lady was made by those photographs, though for years he has told the story as though he was there and he described the smell of the book burning and him breathing in the sting of petrol so that he coughed like a sick dog and the wet Edinburgh streets could not put out the fire of that book.

He imagines setting fire to the file the doctor has on him, all those X-ray pictures of his tarred and tarnished lungs and the records of his test results and the letter saying there is nothing can be done. He sniffs the singed and petrol-stung air, hears the crackle of burning, sees a curl of smoke and the flames blue and yellow and green.

'Aren't black cats supposed to be lucky?' he says to himself, quiet and under his broken breath.

'It will be OK,' he tells his pillar-of-salt wife.

*

A whole crowd pushed into the new picture – the bachelor and the Chinese not-yet-married bride in her white dress and the lovers arm in arm and walking into the picture; and the teenage girls on their mobile phones and a young man in a turquoise-blue zip-up hoodie pulling a heavy suitcase over the sand; and a woman looking for teaspoons or shoes or names she has misplaced – or maybe she looks for the King George half-crown of memory; and men and women of all ages looking up, looking down, looking not in the one place but looking all ways and looking unfocused, even looking confused or lost; and dogs, painted and real; and the boy in drab-coloured clothes – the boy who would one day be a big-name artist and paint pictures about love and folly and time. And Livvy is there, her hair tucked behind one ear and anxiously casting her gaze out of the far right of the picture; the old artist wonders what it is she sees, for there is nothing on the screen on the back of his camera.

And behind the crowd, his crowd, are figures from Giandomenico Tiepolo's crowd, the masked Punchinello in love and fondling an uncrowned dancing woman's breast; men in cocked bicorne and tri-corne hats; a lady in a red dress with a floppy red bonnet that looks like something deflated; and the acrobats, far off and tipping and unbalanced.

And not angels, unless birds flung haphazardly across the thinning blue of the sky might be thought a scattering of angels. And a screaming eagle or hawk that birls through the air above everything, its voice like the sound of breaking glass.

The artist will not look to define the work or to give meaning – his meaning – to the picture. He says, when asked, 'I understand the search for meaning but have come to know that meaning is always specific to the viewer and is something fluid, like the tides in the Venice lagoon, and sometimes the water laps quietly beyond the doors of the Hotel Danieli on the front and at other times overspills and drowns the whole city.'

The Eleventh Picture: Epilogue

(from the Greek 'epilogus', meaning conclusion or additional word)

He remembers a time down in the London Underground and the people pressing and pressing and a woman fell. Maybe she fell or she was seized and thrown to the bottom of some stairs. And there was a man there telling the crowd to get back, to let her breathe, to give her some air. She looked as though she was sleeping. He did not dare think it was more than that. She was not young or pretty, except as we all are in sleep, and her clothes were all out of order and her underclothes were a little exposed. They should not have been looking. It was not decent to look. Hadn't his father always said that it was rude to look like that?

He tried to back away from the sleeping woman but the crowd was tight at his back and stiff as a wall on all sides. It was like being held and not let go. Like lying in bed when he was small and he was in the under-the-covers dark and his brother was sitting where the covers opened and everything tucked in on all sides tight as drums or window putty, and he could not catch his breath and he called out to his brother to let him out, to let him breathe, to give him air.

And now he does not like crowds, the push and pull of them, and the not being able to snatch for breath. And the woman asleep? He wonders if it was only sleep and he wonders what became of her, if she was lifted up and passed over the heads of the crowd and into the light. He's seen that happen at music concerts, though the people surfing the crowd were awake and not anything less than fully alive.

*

They will be exhibited, the pictures, his photographs. In Venice. He lays them out on the floor of his studio and walks around in them and breathes them in. Ten is a round number – that's something his maths teacher would have said. Not perfect, is something he might also have said, for perfect numbers have their own particular qualities. Just rounded.

'And our little life is rounded with a sleep.'

He phones Livvy and says she must come. There is more to do. 'One more picture,' he says. And maybe she hears the urgency in his voice.

*

'Remember when we stood under the pier at Brighton, out of the wind? And you took my hand – I think you did. Only, I do not remember it was you and remember it was my wife and my heart was young again and hammering. And the pebbles slipping beneath my feet so that I looked like an old fool or like someone dancing.'

*

He was on Crosby beach once. To see the drowned men coming back to shore. He watched the tide recede and the rusted bronze men rise up out of the water. It was a moment of some significance, he thought, but he did not want to put it into words, to pin it down like a butterfly specimen in a lidded display case.

'They put the living butterfly in a glass vessel and cotton wool soaked in a heart-stopping sedative and the butterfly slips easy into sleep and just as easy into death. They are called "killing jars", those glass vessels.'

He walked out to stand beside one of the bronze men, shoulder to shoulder and looking out to sea. Do they look with longing? As though they already miss the push and pull of water, like being held in a crowd and now let go. He took one rusted hand in his, felt the roughness of metal that will not last.

Love will last; love is the thing that will survive us – he had not been convinced of that before. He thought maybe his work would be the thing that survived – misunderstood perhaps. Now, remembering that day on Crosby beach, holding the hand of a rusted man, he is not so sure. He is not so sure they can be separated, the love and the work.

*

In the fresco of *Il Mondo Nuovo* the artist Giandomenico Tiepolo weeps. We do not know why he weeps. He has painted his father into the picture, though by this time his father is dead and buried somewhere far off. And there is a woman in the crowd and he loves her like he's never been hurt and he watches her sleep sometimes and he weeps then too. And the people, looking out to sea, looking to their beginning and to their end, he maybe weeps for them also, for there is an uncommon tenderness in his painting of them.

*

'This last picture will not be so complicated as the others, will be something empty, like the curtain coming down on a stage that the actors have long since left. But it will be a conclusion of sorts, too, and something said, the last word.'

Livvy sips from a cup of tea – once it was a blue Royal Worcester porcelain willow-pattern cup; now it is not – and makes small notes in her black book.

'A view under the pier so there is no sky, and looking along the receding length of the pier, like an exercise in perspective, and at the end can be seen something like a hole in the fabric of time and space, a glimpse into infinity, into the eternal.

'And the rusted bronze men from Crosby beach, just their heads and shoulders above the water, and they are being embraced again by the sea; and the acrobats out there too, their human pyramid both balanced and unbalanced and when they fall – and they *will* fall, for even angels fall sometimes – their landing will not be something hard and the sea will catch them and hold them and never give them up.'

'And with or without angels?' Livvy says.

He looks at her funny, as though she is not there, as though she is a thought in his head.

'And a limp cloth,' he says, 'the same that had once carried in the air, adrift like a laundry-day sheet pegged out on a wind-whipped line and it suddenly is unpegged and floats like a thought on the air. But the cloth now dropped out of the sky and it is draped over some structure under the pier, all lift and *luft* taken out of it.'

Luft is the German word for 'air' or 'breath'; it is also, with only a small shift, close to *lutf*, which is an Urdu word meaning 'enjoyment'.

*

Livvy finishes her tea.

There are eleven pictures now and the story feels more rounded than it did with ten and he would like to have told his maths teacher that, shown him what eleven pictures look like. Not perfect but prime.

He coughs and clears his throat, as though he has something important to say.

He pulls a pencil from behind his ear and with a small pocket penknife he whittles it to a new point and takes up a piece of paper and writes something in the centre of the page, writes it with a flourish though the writing is spidery and scrawled.

Livvy looks over his shoulder – or it is his wife who looks. Yes, it must be his wife, for she is so close he can smell the damp earth and overripe apples and the wet end of a cork pulled from a bottle of red wine and the mint of patchouli. All of that. He is certain of it.

On the paper he has written only three words, but they are enough.

It is done.

Acknowledgements

With or Without Angels is a work of fiction and the characters depicted are all a part of that fiction. But that is not to say that the work does not have some link to the real world.

In August of 2021 my wife and I invited Richard Demarco and a friend to our garden for tea and scones and cake. On the day of the afternoon tea Richard had an unexpected house guest, so he phoned ahead to ask if he could also bring her to our garden. It was one of those perfect late summer days with blue sky and sunshine, and though we were troubled a little by wasps, they were not yet inclined to sting. Richard, even in his early nineties, is great company and he regaled us with wonderful stories of art and festivals and artists.

We learned that Richard's house guest had been recently widowed and she told us a little about her late husband. He was a Scottish artist with an international reputation but was not a name I was familiar with. His widow encouraged us to look at his work online when we had the time.

The next day I visited the late artist's online pages. Towards the end of his life he had produced a series of works, photo collages, that he titled *The New World*. He had made a video to accompany this work, in which he discussed his art and his life. He was gentle and eloquent and interesting. And he knew at the time that he was seriously ill.

Over the next few weeks, I listened to that video again and again, at the same time poring over his works. I was deeply touched by the man and by the work he had produced, and I knew I had to write something, was compelled to – not a biographical sketch or an essay on the artist's work, but something creative.

The New World photo collages had been this artist's response to a work by the eighteenth-century artist Giandomenico Tiepolo, a fresco called *Il Mondo Nuovo* that is on display in the Ca' Rezzonico museum in Venice; my work would be a creative response to both.

With or Without Angels was drafted over a single week and then filed in a folder on my computer. I did not know what I was going to do with it. After about a month I decided to send it to the artist's widow. Her response was overwhelming and generous, and she encouraged me to look for a publisher and gave permission for the artist's photo collages to be a part of the work.

The late artist's name is Alan Smith. His artworks and the film he made can both be viewed here: https://www.alansmithartist.com/the-new-world.html.

Thanks to Jill Vites and Richard Demarco and Terry Ann Newman for that wonderful summer afternoon tea in 2021. Thanks to my wife and my family. Thanks to Fairlight Books for risking another book with me – to Louise Boland and Laura Shanahan and the whole Fairlight team. Thanks to Chloe Rosser for help in accessing high-resolution images of Alan Smith's work. And as always thanks to the Demon Beaters of Lumb... you know who you are and why you are to be thanked.

And special thanks to the late Alan Smith for this 'collaboration'.

List of Illustrations

About the Author

Douglas Bruton is the author of three previous novels: *The Chess Piece Magician* (2009), *Mrs Winchester's Gun Club* (2019) and *Blue Postcards* (2021), which was longlisted for the Walter Scott Prize for Historical Fiction. His short fiction has appeared in various publications, including *Northwords Now*, *New Writing Scotland*, *Aesthetica*, *The Fiction Desk* and the *Irish Literary Review*, and has won competitions including Fish and the Neil Gunn Prize. He lives in the Scottish Borders.

About the Artists

Alan Smith (1941–2019) was a Scottish artist who worked extensively as a painter, ceramicist and teacher, exhibiting in Europe and America for a number of years. In 1991, shortly after his fiftieth birthday, the artist made a conscious decision to remove himself from the world of public art. Years later, after being diagnosed with a life-threatening illness, Smith completed a final body of work: *The New World*, prompted by Giandomenico Tiepolo's *Il Mondo Nuovo*.

Giovanni Domenico (Giandomenico) Tiepolo (1727–1804) was an Italian painter and printmaker. Born in Venice, he was the son of the artist Giovanni Battista (Giambattista) Tiepolo. He is known for his portraits and scenes of eighteenth-century Venetian life, including several frescoes, now displayed in the Ca' Rezzonico museum.